I0624939

SNAPSHOTS IN TIME

Twenty Hardscrabble Vignettes

Eric Grate

COAL SHED PUBLISHING

For my Michelle.

REFLECTION

"It's hard work to be happy. " - Brian Wilson

ABOUT THE AUTHOR

Eric Grate was born and raised in Greenfield, Ohio. He graduated from Edward Lee McClain High School in 1984 and is a United States Marine Corps veteran. He had a twenty-year career as a Quality Engineer in the automotive industry before embarking on a ten-year career as a professional photographer in 2009. In 2018, Eric founded Big Jack's Coffeehouse & Cafe, which has two locations in Lawrenceburg, KY. Eric and his wife, Michelle, reside in Danville, KY with their mean cat, Boo Radley.

CONTENTS

INTRODUCTION

I wrote this book for thinkers. I know, I know. Every book is written for thinkers, right? After all, if a person cannot think, he cannot read. That is a fair statement and, on the surface, it is true. This book, however, is different.

In comparison, most works of fiction have all of the elements of a plot: protagonist, antagonist, and conflict; with a beginning, a middle, and an end. This book, on the other hand, is a collection of vignettes. A vignette may contain conflict. It most likely includes a protagonist and maybe an antagonist. However, it does not have a beginning, middle, or end. It is simply a snapshot in time. Hence the title of this book. Whereas a traditional work of fiction tells the reader a complete story, a vignette simply gives them a brief glimpse of one moment in a larger story and encourages them to interpret what they have read. This allows them to fill in the gaps and decide for themselves what the bigger picture looks like. The beauty of the whole thing is that a dozen people can read the same vignette and come away with a dozen interpretations of what they just read.

I first considered writing a book like this about a year ago after reading Ernest Hemingway's 1924 book of vignettes entitled *in our time* (all lowercase), commonly referred to as *in our time - The 1924 Paris Edition.* This was Hemingway's first published work of fiction, and he was experimenting with his style of English prose and helping to define the early stages of American literary modernism. Hemingway was a young man in 1924, just turning twenty-five, and he was 'finding his voice' you might say. As I write this, I just turned fifty-nine and am already comfortable with my voice. This book is how I have decided to share it with you.

Snapshots In Time contains twenty vignettes that provide a brief glimpse of life as it unfolds for otherwise unremarkable people. As you begin reading, you might wonder why the story is incomplete. It's then that I ask you to switch from reader to thinker and complete the stories to your satisfaction. You separate the heroes from the villains. You decide who wins and who loses. You choose how you want to feel about what you just read. Make the stories go where you want them to go. Most of all, have fun and enjoy!

Eric Grate

October 20, 2024

'B OUT NO PAIN

The wounded man grimaced as he climbed down from the back of the truck and sat in the oversized, worn, red recliner outside the medical tent.

"He don't care 'bout no pain," the big man driving the truck told the doctor.

"Excuse me?" The doctor replied, looking up from his clipboard.

"Don't worry 'bout shootin' him full of painkillers or puttin' him in no hospital. There ain't no time for that. Just patch him up. We need him back in the line," the big man said, gesturing with a nod to the string of defensive positions that stretched for miles along the west bank of Paint Creek.

"Don't be ridiculous," the annoyed doctor mumbled under his breath while removing the soldier's soiled bandages. The wound was severely infected, and it gave off a putrid odor that hovered in the hot July air. The doctor had no antibiotics to administer and guessed the man would die within a few weeks.

The driver stepped out of the truck and eyed the doctor warily. When the doctor started to speak again, the big man spat a stream of tobacco juice onto the dusty ground at the doctor's feet. The doctor paused and considered the situation as the low rumble of a distant artillery barrage floated through the camp. "Orderly!" He called.

A gaunt young man in baggy clothes stepped from the medical tent. "Yessir?"

"Clean and dress this man's wound," the doctor ordered. "Motrin for pain."

The wounded man did not say what course of action he preferred, and no one bothered to ask him.

PURPLE DRANK

They were fucked up. All of them.

The Kennedy kid resembled a corpse stretched out on his back with his head hanging over the arm of the couch; mouth wide open.

Glenny White lay curled up in a ball, naked and shivering, in a puddle of piss on the kitchen floor.

Slumped in a rocking chair with a lap full of vomit, tapping her fingers on her forehead, was a young Bohemian girl whom everyone knew as Spinner. She whispered the alphabet over and over and over again. Strangely, she forgot the letter E each time she recited it.

Gatewood walked in and surveyed the scene. He snorted hard, cleared his throat, and spat a thick mass of green phlegm towards the open window. The foul wad hit the bottom trim around the window and ran slowly down the wall.

The ugly dog got up from his position by the fireplace, went to the window to investigate, sniffed the gooey mess, and promptly licked it up.

My gag reflex kicked in, and I swallowed hard to avoid puking.

"What the fuck, Butter? You gross sumbitch. What the hell's wrong with you?" Gatewood asked the dog, who licked his lips and resumed his position by the fireplace.

"May we please continue?" I asked.

Gatewood lit a cigarette. "Where was we?"

S WEETIE

When Marty came out of the restroom, two men were sitting at the table next to his. Both were in their mid-thirties, big guys with beards and tattoos, dressed in denim, flannel, and work boots; not the hipster kind either. If Jackson City had a steel mill or a coal mine, these were just the type of men who would work there.

"Hey, guys. You doin' okay today?" Marty said to the two men before sitting down.

The men looked at Marty and grinned. "Doin' just fine, sweetie," one of them replied.

Marty felt his face turning red.

When the waitress brought his beer, Marty drank it slowly, determined to finish it at his leisure regardless of the two men sitting beside him. He was not stupid though and he was equally determined to keep to himself as long as the situation allowed it.

E MERGENCY ROOM BATMAN

It was quiet for a Friday night. We had seen a baby with an ear infection, a teenage girl complaining of stomach cramps, and a man from the textile plant who sprained his ankle when he tripped over a pallet. None of the typical Friday night visitors, though. No drunk drivers, no drug overdoses, no housewives sporting fat lips and bruised arms from being clumsy. It was a little weird.

Things got interesting though around ten o'clock when a thoroughly annoyed woman burst through the door with her seven-year-old son in tow. The boy had a gash on his forehead, sustained from nose diving off his parent's bed into the corner of their dresser.

"He's bashed his head clear open!" The boy's mother exclaimed.

The boy was bleeding like a stuck pig, but when I took him and his mother into an examination room and sat him on the table, he was as calm as could be. He wasn't crying, nor did he act like he was in any pain at all. It was as if he didn't know his head was cut open, or he just didn't care.

The boy's jaws were packed with Atomic Fireballs, which he sucked on incessantly. He wore Batman pajamas with black socks pulled up to his knees like boots. He had a pillowcase pinned around his neck for a cape, and a cap pistol tucked into the waistband of his pajama bottoms. Blood had run down his face and soaked into the neck and right shoulder of his pajama top, giving him a maniacal appearance.

A few minutes passed before Doc White came in, his breath smelling of Camel cigarettes, Old Grandad, and Listerine. Doc gave the wound a quick glance, then sewed it shut with seven stitches while the kid's mom prayed to Jesus.

I'll be damned, but that little Batman never shed a tear. I mean he didn't make one sound.

G OODNIGHT, WILLIAM

Last night, as I was leaving work, two of the ER nurses, Sue, a rail-thin redhead with a nose like a hawk, and Alice, a good-looking blonde in her early thirties with big tits and a dirty mouth, were standing outside the door talking and smoking cigarettes. "Goodnight, ladies," I said as I made my way down the steps.

"Goodnight, William," Alice said. "You sleep tight tonight, hunny. Okay?"

My mind flashed to images of Alice and me rolling around on the sheets in some sleazy motel room.

"You're still working out and liftin' them weights, ain't you, William? It shows when you walk. You keep that up, baby. You hear?"

Alice and Sue giggled, and my cheeks burned as I walked to my car. For a moment, I considered waiting around until Alice's shift ended, but I was tired and gave myself a raincheck.

When I got to my car, I looked back at the two nurses. Alice smiled and waved gently with her fingers as a lazy cloud of white smoke drifted into the air from her parted lips.

Pulling away, I smiled back and tried to look unbothered.

A SIMPLE DEATH

The young soldier was dying. His wound, had he been evacuated to the hospital in Danville with the others, would not have been fatal. Of course it was a severe wound, but it would not have taken his life had he received even rudimentary treatment. That much can be said with certainty. As it was, though, the young soldier had not been evacuated. He had fallen near a stone fence, running along the creek at the western edge of the horse farm, and was lying in a deep rut in tall grass so as not to be visible to the stretcher-bearers who canvassed the battlefield once the fighting had moved off further north. He had tried to call out, but the pain was too great to produce much more than a whisper. After the ambulances were loaded, he heard them leaving along the Lebanon Pike. Once they were gone, he was left alone with the dead, his lifeblood soaking into the Earth.

The soldier could hear scattered small arms

fire in the distance. His comrades, no doubt, clearing out the last few pockets of enemy resistance.

He thought of his mother and father, his sister, Jane, and his dog, Rascal. He also thought of the girl in London that had he spent three days with during the advance from Knoxville, but he could not recall her name.

The breeze blew cool across the soldier's face and brought with it the smell of horses and fresh-cut hay. He grew weak. As he lay there, his thoughts turned to some of the great men throughout history who had died in battle. Men like James IV, Vlad the Impaler, Davy Crocket, J.E.B. Stuart, George Custer, The Red Barron, Enver Pasha, Doris Miller, and many others.

If only I had someone here with me, he thought. *Someone to cry. Someone to write down my last words. Someone to mourn at my passing. It would be a beautiful death, a noble death, had I someone to share it with.*

But, he was alone. He would die a simple death instead.

N ANA'S NAP

"So, Charlie, how about breakfast?"

"Yay!" Three-year-old Charlie exclaimed as he bounced into the living room and dug into the box of toys by the couch.

Nana went to the kitchen and prepared hot chocolate and cinnamon toast, then sat Charlie at the little wooden table by the back door. She cut the two slices of cinnamon toast into four squares each and filled a small plastic cup with hot chocolate before sprinkling a few marshmallows on top. "You eat breakfast while Nana works in the garden. Okay, sweetie?"

"Okay," Charlie answered.

"You'll be able to see me out the window. When I'm finished, we can watch *Fraggle Rock*."

Nana walked onto the back porch and closed the kitchen door behind her. The brightly colored gardening gloves hanging out of her back pocket caught Charlie's eye, and he recited the colors out loud, "Purple, yell-row, red, blue, green!"

Charlie poked at the marshmallows in his cup with a toy soldier, took a sip of hot chocolate, and ate a square of cinnamon toast with one bite. He sang a few lines of "Fraggle Rock", then counted his fingers: "One, two, free, five, eight, nine, ten!"

Nana pulled on her gloves, grabbed the small garden fork out of her basket, got down on her knees, and started probing for tulip bulbs in the soil around the big rock in her flower garden.

Nana was seventy-two years old, with shoulder-length gray hair she kept pinned back on the sides. She was a little thick around the middle and had battled high blood pressure for years, but she was in good shape for a woman her age. Daily walks through the woods behind her house and time spent tending the various flowers, shrubs, and bushes around her yard kept her active.

Charlie busied himself with the things that three-year-olds find necessary and interesting. First, he dipped his fingers in his hot chocolate and painted the top of his small table. Next, he talked to Nana's cat, Dust Bunny, and wouldn't have been too surprised had she responded. Then he took all the toys out of the toy box and scattered them about the floor for a myriad of reasons known only to him. Mostly though, he watched Nana work amongst her flowers, selecting just the right tool from her basket to dig, snip, clip, prune, or cut. He watched her dig up bulbs, gather blooms, pull weeds, turn dirt, spread fertilizer, and water select plants with her can.

When Nana made a funny face and knelt on the ground, Charlie laughed and clapped his hands. When she lay on her back for a nap, Charlie returned to his breakfast and waited for her to get up.

INTO THE NIGHT

When I get to the traffic light at Washington Street, I consider turning left and going to Stewart's for a beer. I even go so far as to switch on my left turn signal. But as soon as the light turns green, I make a right.

It's almost midnight, and the streets are empty. Most of the houses are dark, but flickering television screens light up a few windows along the way. Night shifters, most likely, eating leftovers and watching the last few minutes of a John Wayne western they've seen a hundred times before.

As I turn onto Summerfield Street, Fred Pollock staggers out the door of The Pad Cafe, followed by a few notes from a steel guitar. I consider pulling over and offering him a ride home, but I've been banging his big-ass German wife, Elsa, every Thursday afternoon for the past few months, and I feel like it would be weird to have him in the car. So I let him walk.

Turning onto Second Street, I see the bathroom light go out at our house. I decide to give the old lady a few minutes to get to bed before I go in, so I park the Beetle at the curb and light a Chesterfield from the pack over the sun visor. The cool breeze coming through the window feels good, though it's tinged with the pungent odor of the slaughterhouse across the railroad tracks.

Fred Pollock wobbles by, and I sink down in my seat to watch as he stops under the streetlight and pisses into the sewer grate before turning down Paint Street towards his house.

"That was Looking Glass singing about that fine girl, Brandy. She'll make some lucky guy a good wife one day. If he can keep her out of the bars, that is. The best music all summer long. WLS 890 Chicago! Broadcasting all over the country, not to mention Canada and probably Mars. Definitely Uranus. John Records Landecker here. Records is truly my middle name. I have the paper to prove it, you know. It's almost time for Boogie Check. But first, here's the Edgar Winter Group with 'Frankenstein.' It's alive! Alive!"

I roll up the window and step out of the car. It's eerily quiet except for the hum of the streetlight and the distant sound of a car going over the bridge on Route 28 a mile away. Raven, our old black cat, walks off the porch and rubs against my leg before making her way into the night.

A lonely feeling comes over me. I take a long

last drag off my cigarette and flick it across the street. Then, I unlock the door and go inside.

TWO PROFESSIONALS

Three men sat in a coffeehouse on a side street two blocks from downtown. Two of the men, both professionals, one in his early forties and the other in his late twenties, sat in armchairs by the window. The third, an older man seventy-five or eighty years old, sat at a table in the back.

"See the old man at that table?" the older professional said, nodding towards the back of the coffeehouse.

The younger professional turned and looked at the old man.

"He's a people watcher. He sits there every day and analyzes everyone that comes in here. Writes it all down in a notebook."

"Oh yeah? Why?" Said the younger professional, glancing again at the old man.

"He has nothing else to do."

The younger professional laughed. "That's a

little strange. I wonder what kind of stuff he writes?"

"He profiles people based on the coffee they order."

"How do you know? Have you seen his book?"

"Yes," the older professional said. "He left it on his table once when he went to the men's room. I flipped through a few pages."

"What did it say?"

"He wrote that I always ordered cappuccinos in the morning, macchiatos in the afternoons, and Americanos in the evening. He noted that I prefer a real cup over a paper one, and I never add sugar to my drinks. He called me a *"cultured man"* and indicated that I was *"well-traveled."*

"Well, he isn't wrong," the younger professional said.

"I guess not. He has a long list of people who drink designer coffee on ice with whipped cream, syrup, and sprinkles. He claims they don't really like coffee. They like sugar and milk. Ordering it with a little coffee makes them feel sophisticated."

"That's pretty funny!"

"He also has written extensively on lesbians and white liberals, his words not mine, who cycle through nondairy creamers, depending on what's popular at the time. Ten years ago, it was soy milk; no one except faux hippy college professors drinks that nowadays, according to him. Then almond milk, and finally, starting a couple of years ago, oat milk."

"Soy boys!" the younger professional

exclaimed.

"Get this. He wrote that Father Michael, from Saint Pete's, prefers cream in his coffee, but he drinks it black as a form of self-flagellation."

"What does the old man drink?" The young professional asked.

"I don't know. I've never bothered to notice."

"What would he say about me drinking decaf?"

"He'd probably say it's the coffee equivalent of a fake I.D."

Both of the men laughed.

"Don't turn around," the younger professional said, "but he keeps looking at us. He's writing as fast as he can."

The older professional smiled. "Let's order another coffee. Something different. We'll try to throw him off our trail."

T HE KING IS DEAD

The boy had been pulling his little brothers (the twins) up and down the sidewalk in a red wagon when his mother stepped out onto the porch and gave him the news.

The boy heard what his mother said but had difficulty accepting that what she told him was even plausible, much less accurate.

Saying the King was dead was like saying the Moon had fallen from the sky. It was highly improbable. No, it was more than that. It was impossible.

A TIME OF TRANSITION

(T) "Let's pick up where we left off last week."

(E) "Where was that?"

(T) "You were telling me about your life after dropping out of college. You said it was a...let me see. Here it is. You said, *'It was a time of transition.'*"

(E) "I had a strange mindset then."

(T) "How so?"

(E) "You're a woman. You wouldn't understand."

(T) "I might."

(E) "I would go through these cycles."

(T) "What kind of cycles?"

(E) "Well, I'd party my ass off for a while. I mean, like every day for several weeks. Alcohol, weed, pills, women. Then, after a period of partying and self-indulgence, I'd go into a fitness and intellectual phase where I would give up drinking, weed, cigarettes, and women while I concentrated on exercising and reading. It was like an obsession. After work, I'd go home and lift weights for an hour, then run five miles. I'd eat canned chicken and raw vegetables, then spend hours reading. Classics like *Moby Dick, A Farewell To Arms, Huckleberry Finn,* and *Don Quixote.* This would last for a couple weeks, then I would cycle back to drinking, smoking, and women. That went on through most of my twenties."

(T) "What do you think triggered the transitions from one phase to another?"

(E) "I was thinking too much."

(T) "About what?"

(E) "Being something I wasn't. I always wanted to write poetry, sketch landscapes, make portraits of interesting faces, and speak words people wanted to hear."

(T) "What's kept you from doing it?"

(E) "Lack of talent."

(T) "How do you know you lack talent? Have you ever tried doing any of those things?"

(E) "Not really. People like me don't do that stuff."

(T) "What do people like you do?"

(E) "We get by."

T HE CATNAPPERS

It was a little past midnight when Jack Connor pulled his '75 Chevelle slowly off the road and onto the gravel drive in front of a row of abandoned chicken coops. Screech Becker was riding shotgun; Donnie Kessler, Bryan Drake, and Ronnie Aquino were in the backseat.

The boys piled out of the car, and each, as if on cue, found his own tree or bush to pee on. When finished, they walked stealthily back down Miami Trace Road, fifty feet to the Maple Valley Country Club. They were trying to be quiet, but the Boone's Farm they had drank was betraying them. They laughed, said "sssssssshhhhhhhhhhhhhhhhhh!" over and over again with one finger pressed to their lips, and issued constant reminders for the others to "shut the fuck up" in a loud voice.

The Catnappers' mission was to relieve the

clubhouse bar of its supply of liquor, cigars, Beer Nuts, and Slim Jims. Confidence was high as this was not the first raid the boys had conducted against this very target.

A car approached, and they all dropped down in the ditch behind tall grass and weeds until the car passed. Then, with Screech in the lead, they scrambled through the open gate, up the blacktop driveway, then off to the left into a patch of small Maple trees they called the "front woods." The Catnappers were in position.

The operation was a risky one. Pulling it off required a stealthy approach from the front woods to the seventh fairway, followed by a low crawl across thirty yards of manicured grass, a careful walk across the gravel cart path, and a quiet climb through a window with a broken lock. Not an easy task for a group of intoxicated teenagers. Lastly, they had to avoid waking Tim Beverly, the club pro who lived in a single-wide trailer just forty yards from the clubhouse.

HE WAS A JEW

"How'd they kill him?" Gary asked.

"Shot him," John answered.

"Any idea why they did it?"

"He was a Jew," said John.

The waitress stopped at the table with a pot of coffee. Gary sat his cup down so she could refill it.

"More coffee, John?" The waitress asked.

"No, I'm good, Eileen. Thanks."

"What does he being a Jew have to do with it?" Gary asked.

"It shouldn't have anything to do with it. But, it does," John said.

"Why?"

"Hating Jews is just a way of life for some."

Gary looked deep into his coffee cup and did not respond.

John continued. "No people in the history of the world have suffered like the Jews."

Gary thought for a moment. "I guess you're

right. I wonder why?"

"Because they're God's chosen people," said John.

"The Jews are God's chosen people?"

"Sure they are. Don't you read your Bible?"

Gary shrugged. "It's been a while."

"Deuteronomy. Chapter seven. Verse six. It's all there."

"So, some bastard shot an old man because he was one of God's chosen people? Man, oh man," Gary said, shaking his head.

"And because our so-called leaders need us regular folks to be enemies with one another."

"What do you mean?"

"Identity politics," John answered. "Obama started it and every Democrat politician in the country got thier marching orders from him."

Gary nodded.

"They divide us by race, religion, sex, income, sexual orientation, ethnic background, political party, you name it, my friend. Anything to keep us at odds with each other. Before you know it, hating your enemy isnt that hard. Even if he really isn't your enemy at all."

"What the hell is going to stop it?" Gary asked.

John started to speak, then sat back and motioned for the waitress. "Eileen, you better put on another pot of coffee."

H OPPER'S CHOICE

Hopper stood on the roof's ledge and gazed up at the crescent moon hanging in the sky. The moon seemed to beckon him, and Hopper longed to respond. Moreso out of loneliness than out of want. He imagined the moon was a recliner, and he envisioned his mother sitting in it, looking down at him and laughing. *"Come on, Hoppy. Come and join Mommy."*

Hopper drained the beer from the can in his hand and tossed it aside before scooting forward ever so slowly until the toes of his worn boots extended a full three inches past the ledge. Looking down, he noticed how the intersecting lines separating the sections created specific points on the sidewalk. *"Just pick a point and go for it, Hoppy!"*

Mary Middleton had only been in the ground since Monday afternoon, but Hopper missed her already. He hated her complaining and her sarcasm and her meanness and her negativity. But now that she was gone, he missed it. *How wierd is that?*

Hopper didn't really take much after his mother. Unlike her, he was happy most of the time. Maybe happy is too strong of a word. Let's say he was content. He rarely complained, but due to the fate of having been born her son, he suffered from every one of her setbacks, failures, and poor decisions, just like she did. In fact, he suffered more because, unlike her, he wasn't numb. He felt the sting. But was the sting really so terrible? *It's better than feeling nothing*, he thought.

Hopper closed his eyes, stretched his arms out from his sides, and turned his face skyward to the crescent moon. Then, he began to count, "One, two, three, four, five..." When he reached one hundred, he would make his choice.

D YSTOPIA

"I'm joining' up in April. Soon as I turn seventeen," Cooper said proudly.

"No, you ain't neither," Kevin said, looking up from his plate. "This war's windin' down, and there ain't no need for you to run off and get yourself killed for no reason."

Cooper shook his head and laughed. "You been sayin' the war's windin' down for two years. I'm joinin' the militia, and there ain't nobody gonna stop me."

"Listen, Coop. It ain't no game." Kevin said. "At Fairview, we got pinned down by snipers. They was hidin' up in the city hall clock tower and the steeple of the Methodist Church. It took us three hours to get 'em cleared out. We lost a lot of good men."

"Those goddamn bastards!" Cooper seethed.

"The old man wanted to send a message. So, he had us bring fifty prisoners to the center of town. We lined 'em up against the courthouse wall five at a time, and shot 'em. Just like that," Kevin said, snapping his fingers.

Cooper's face lit up. "Was it a firin' squad, or did ya'll machine gun em? Did you have to pop any in the head with a pistol?

Kevin didn't answer.

"How many did YOU kill, Kev?" Cooper persisted, wide-eyed and eager for details. "Tell me, Kev. How many of them sons a bitches did you git?"

Kevin stood up from the table, turned his back to his brother, and walked to the stove. He rubbed his hands together and held them, palms out towards the heat, trying to warm them. It took him several seconds to respond to Cooper's question. "Three. Four maybe. No more'n six."

T HE NEAR DEATH OF A YOUNG SALESMAN

Mrs. Van Dorn watched the young salesman through the living room window. He sat his big leather case on the porch, adjusted his tie, popped a peppermint into his mouth, and knocked on the door.

"It's open!" Mrs. Van Dorn called from the sofa.

Picking up his case, the young salesman opened the door and stepped inside while removing his hat. Fixing his eyes on Mrs. Van Dorn, the young salesman smiled broadly and said, "Good morning, ma'am. My name is Benja…"

"Stop right there, friend," Mr. Van Dorn said, while stepping out of the bathroom, bare-chested, his face half-covered with shaving cream.

The young salesman was startled but did not lose his composure. "Good morning, sir. I am Benjamin Lyle Pfister, and I represent the Dover Sup…"

Mr. Van Dorn produced a large revolver from the holster on his hip and pointed it toward the young salesman. "Pick up that case and get outta my house. Otherwise, you'll be coolin' on a slab down at Foley's while I'm having breakfast."

The young salesman froze.

"I ain't kiddin', mister. I'll blow your damned head clean off."

With that, the young salesman put on his hat and backed away slowly, out the door, and off the porch. Then he ran up the street, dragging his big leather case behind, and looking over his shoulder as he went.

"Why'd you scare that poor young salesman so, Earl?" Mrs. Van Dorn asked her husband. "I was curious to know what he had in that big old leather case."

Mr. Van Dorn eyed his wife up and down. "Get my breakfast ready," he said. "I got things to do. And put some clothes on, for crying out loud."

S LUMMIN'

There were five of us packed into the Civic. Kurt was driving, Patty was riding bitch, I was in the back seat behind Kurt, Bob sat behind Patty, and Tammy sat squeezed between Bob and me with her head resting on my shoulder. We were all either drunk or high. I was probably both, and I know Bob was.

Kurt turned onto Oak Street, and as we crossed the bridge, he lowered the volume on the radio and announced that we were entering the slums. He said that everyone should lock their doors and, for good measure, he advised the girls to keep their legs tightly closed. He sounded like Walter Cronkite breaking into the regularly scheduled programming with a special report.

The back of my neck began to burn, and I felt my fists clench into balls. I wanted to punch Kurt in the back of the head as we passed my family's house, but I held myself back and slumped down in my seat. Kurt was taking a swipe at me for dating his sister. It was his only card, and I let him play it.

H OT AND SWEATY

It was hot in the room.

An old man, a young man, and a middle-aged woman sat on creaky wooden chairs, waiting for their names to be called.

The air conditioning had stopped working four days ago, and an old box fan sat in the open window, working to the point of exhaustion, trying to cool the room even a little. Its efforts were to no avail, and the young man cursed the fan and damned it to Hell.

"This would have been normal when I was a kid," the old man said. "Just a part of life."

"What a miserable life," the young man replied.

"I remember when my parents bought our first AC," the middle-aged woman said while slowly fanning herself with yesterday's paper. "I was fifteen years old. It was a big window unit they put in the hallway upstairs. They only ran it at night, and we all opened our bedroom doors so the cool air could get in. I don't remember it helping much."

"We used to sleep on the living floor when it was scorching hot," the old man said. "We opened the windows and let the breeze in, if there was one. If it weren't a school night, Mom would let us sleep outside on the front porch or in a tent in the backyard."

The young man glared at the old man. "What the hell did that do?" It sounded more like a statement than it did a question.

"Just a way to make being hot and sweaty kinda fun, I guess," the old man answered.

"For Christ's sake," the young man said with a dismissive grin that was more aggressive than engaging. "I can think of better ways to have fun getting hot and sweaty," he continued, staring at the middle-aged woman.

"My childhood summers were a never-ending string of hot, sweaty nights," the middle-aged woman said.

The young man watched a bead of sweat run down the middle-aged woman's neck and linger briefly before disappearing under her white blouse. He opened his mouth to speak but stopped when he noticed the old man reaching into the tool bag beside his chair.

N INE HUNDRED DOLLARS

My name is Angela DuVall. I was born Margaret Mullins in Greenfield, Ohio, on Easter Sunday, 1934, in a shack on Smith Street behind Charlie Cohen's junkyard. My father was a hobo from Bluefield, Virginia, who spent a week in Greenfield during the summer of 1933, helping to put a new roof on the Methodist Church. My mother said his name was Harvin. It's unclear if that was his first name, or last name, or if it was even his name at all.

Mother cleaned house and washed laundry for some of the local well-to-dos and managed to move us into a rental on the corner of Fourth and Lyndon when I was six years old.

I graduated from McClain High School in 1951, and a few weeks later, Mother sent me off to Columbus to live with a rich man named Gordon Montgomery and his wife, Claudia. I was seventeen, and Gordon was forty-four. Later, I discovered that he paid my mother nine hundred dollars for me.

The Montgomerys lived in a big house on the

east side of Columbus with another girl Gordon had acquired the same way he got me. Her name was Annette, and she was twenty years old, although she looked much younger. She was from Richmond, Indiana.

Gordon and Claudia were very good to us. They bought us expensive clothes, shoes, makeup, and jewelry. They ensured we had the latest French lingerie and perfumes. They had our hair styled like Hollywood movie stars, our teeth whitened, and we got regular manicures and pedicures. They sent us to Miss Francis Tisdale's Finishing School for a year, where we learned proper etiquette, how to walk and talk like a lady, and how to host social gatherings for the elite class. They even hired tutors From Franklin College to instruct us in literature, music, art, philosophy, rhetoric, and geography.

In the evenings, Gordon and Claudia trained us in the more practical skills related to our assigned vocation.

WALKING WITH RUBE

Tommy wouldn't shut up about the big old drunk gal he had balled over the hood of his car in the alley behind Mama Rosa's the night before.

"I'm telling ya, Milt, that broad was so ugly she could make onions cry. I swear to God. She entered an ugly contest, and they said, 'Sorry, no professionals.' Ain't that some shit?" Tommy said, slapping his knee and laughing with his mouth wide open.

"Did she have a name?" I asked.

Tommy looked at me blankly. "Did she have a name? How the hell would I know her name? She moved that big old ass like a professional. That's all I cared about. Get this, she had a boil the size of an egg on her rump, and every time she slowed down, I poked it with my finger and she'd start moving again! Every man should ride one like that at least once in his lifetime."

About five miles out of town, Rube turned off

the main road, drove a half mile down a winding, potholed driveway back to the old Wilson mansion, and parked under a big walnut tree.

Tommy kept right on talking as Jerry and Rube got out of the car. Rube stood back while Jerry came around and opened the rear door.

"Tommy," Jerry said.

Tommy paused his story and turned to Jerry. "Yeah, Boss? What's up? I was just telling..."

"Go with Rube, Tommy."

"Huh?" Tommy looked at Jerry, then at Rube. "What for?" He asked. "What's going on, Jer?"

Tommy turned back to me, but I stared straight ahead, trying to be invisible. I thought maybe I should look at him and say, *It's gonna be okay, Tommy. It'll all work out.* But I didn't. It felt like an eternity before he looked away.

"Come on now," Jerry said.

"You're joking, right? You're messing with me, right Jer?" Said Tommy.

I could feel Tommy's fear. It was damp and cold, and it penetrated my bones.

"Be a big boy now. Okay?" Jerry said.

Tommy started to speak, but his voice gave out. He cleared his throat and whispered, "Do I have to? Please say I don't have to."

Jerry didn't respond.

Tommy took a deep breath and exhaled, trying to compose himself.

"Don't make this any harder than it already is, kid," said Jerry.

Finally, Tommy climbed out of the car.

Jerry pointed to a clump of trees about thirty yards in the distance, and Tommy started in their direction. Rube followed behind, his hands deep in the pockets of his overcoat.

There was something about the way Tommy walked that horrified me. His gate wasn't fluid. It was as if his joints were all gummed up. His movements were jerky and deliberate, and his lanky frame seemed to be made up of sharply defined right angles. It was very disconcerting, and I have never been able to erase that image from my memory.

Jerry leaned back against the car and lit a cigarette. His hands shook, and he nearly dropped his lighter.

I heard Tommy appealing to Rube's good nature as they continued towards the clump of trees. Sammy Miller had made the same appeal when he took the walk last April, and it made me feel like my insides were gonna run right outta my ass. Rube didn't respond.

"Listen," Jerry said, sucking on his cigarette like a fat kid sucking on a Blow Pop. "This ain't what I wanted. Fuckin' Tommy! That prick didn't leave me no other choice."

Jerry wanted validation and he waited for me to tell him he was right. But I just sat there looking straight ahead. The silence pierced the air like a dart.

ACKNOWLEDGEMENT

My sincere thanks to those that engage with me on my blog and social media, give me honest feedback, encourage me when my creative tank is empty, and buy my books. Without you, I would't be able to do this.

BOOKS BY THIS AUTHOR

The Streets Of Greenfield

"The Streets of Greenfield," released in 2023, is a collection of seventeen linked short stories set in the small Appalachian town of Greenfield, OH, between 1946 and 2023. The stories cut against the grain in an edgy, often humorous, style the author calls "hardscrabble fiction."

Experience life on Greenfield's tough streets, where losers sometimes win, winners often lose, and antiheroes carry the day. There is no limit to what goes down on the streets of Greenfield.